WITHDRAW

# Quick, Slow, Mango!

### Anik McGrory

BLOOMSBURY

NEW YORK BERLIN LONDON SYDNEY

First published in the United States of America in January 2011 by Bloomsbury Books for Young Readers
www.bloomsburykids.com

For information about permission to reproduce selections from this book, write to
Permissions, Bloomsbury BFYR, 175 Fifth Avenue, New York, New York 10010

Library of Congress Cataloging-in-Publication Data
McGrory, Anik.
Quick, slow, mango! / Anik McGrory.
p.    cm.
Summary: Kidogo the elephant's mother is always urging him to hurry up, while PolePole the monkey's mother cautions her to slow down, but together they learn that slow and fast can both be good.
ISBN 978-1-59990-242-5 (hardcover)  •  ISBN 978-1-59990-592-1 (reinforced)
[1. Speed—Fiction. 2. Elephants—Fiction. 3. Monkeys—Fiction. 4. Africa—Fiction.]  I. Title.
PZ7.M173Qui 2011          [E]—dc22          2010025975

Art created with pencil and watercolor  •  Typeset in Fink Heavy and Cooper Old Style Light  •  Book design by John Candell

Printed in China by C&C Offset Printing Co., Ltd., Shenzhen, Guangdong
(hardcover) 10 9 8 7 6 5 4 3 2 1
(reinforced) 10 9 8 7 6 5 4 3 2 1

All papers used by Bloomsbury Publishing, Inc.,
are natural, recyclable products made from wood
grown in well-managed forests. The manufacturing
processes conform to the environmental
regulations of the country of origin.

Note:
The word *kidogo* means *little* in Kiswahili; it is pronounced kee-DOE-go.

*Pole, pole* means *slowly, slowly* and is often used to remind people to take their time; it is pronounced POH-lay POH-lay.

*Chapu, chapu* means *hurry, hurry!* It is pronounced CHA-poo CHA-poo.

*For Solenn, who takes on life at full speed*

It was time for breakfast. Kidogo stood on the bank of the winding river, picking up stones and dropping them gently into the water.

"Hurry, hurry!" flapped his mama with her ears. "*Chapu, chapu!* It's time to drink, little one, or you'll be thirsty later."

Kidogo gathered his trunk and
slipped slowly down the riverbank.
On his way, he found a butterfly . . .

. . . and a stick.

He stretched his trunk.

And he said hello to a passing snail.

"Hurry, hurry," his mama called again. "Drink up now, or else we might miss breakfast."

Not far away, PolePole the monkey zipped
past her family, shooting through the grass.
"Mama, Mama! Watch me run!"
"Slowly, slowly, PolePole!" warned her mama.

But her warning came too late. PolePole's
tail tangled in her feet. She tripped and rolled
and bumped her nose. *Ooof!*

"Slowly slowly might be better," she agreed.

Then PolePole spotted mangoes in a tree nearby. She rushed to grab all the ones she could reach. But while she rushed, she didn't hold on well.

And the mangoes slipped and fell.

As more and more mangoes fell, PolePole scrambled to pick them faster and faster.

But as she picked faster and faster,
more and more mangoes fell!

Down at the river, Kidogo had arrived at the water's edge and was just reaching for a drink. But his mama stomped. "Chapu, chapu! Hurry, little one," she said. "Now it's time to graze."

So Kidogo turned around and stumbled along to catch up. He didn't take a drink.

On his way he said
good-bye to the snail.

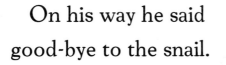

He climbed a hill.

He sat in a hole.

He was pretending to be a rock when his
mama called again, "Chapu, chapu! Eat up
now before the day's too hot!"

But the day was already too hot.
Kidogo licked his dry lips.

He fanned himself with
a floppy leaf.

He sniffed for water.

He was very thirsty. He watched his mama move away
through the tall grass and he turned back toward the river.

Slowly Kidogo waded into the cool water. He
splashed and made waves. He sprayed at the sky.
He took a deep drink.

He admired the mangoes floating past.

Meanwhile, high in the uppermost branches of her tree, PolePole dashed at the very last mango. It flew through the air. And so did PolePole.

The monkey and the mango
splashed into the water together.

She rushed and dove after
that very last mango, but it
only bobbed away.

She swiped at another mango.
It bobbed away too.

Kidogo watched the funny monkey bobbing down the river swiping at the mangoes.

Slowly, slowly.
He waded deeper.

He found a stick.

He stretched his trunk.

He pretended he was a rock . . .

And a mango floated down the river
and stopped for him.
PolePole floated down the river and
stopped for him too.

PolePole watched the funny
elephant waiting very still with
mangoes piling up around him.

She admired the bobbing
mangoes. She stopped very still
and waited. Slowly, slowly.

She wiggled her fingers and
stretched them. She pretended
she was a branch.

And a mango stopped for her.

Kidogo and PolePole sat on the riverbank
slowly munching mangoes.

Mama monkey looked down in approval.

"Yes, PolePole—slowly, slowly."

But Kidogo's mama came searching for Kidogo. "Chapu, chapu, Kidogo! Where can you be? You're very late to eat."

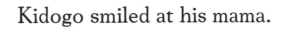

Kidogo smiled at his mama.

He handed her a mango.

And offered her a hug.

Mama saw PolePole. Mama saw the mangoes. And
Mama hugged Kidogo back. "Yes, Kidogo, sometimes
slowly slowly can also be just right."

 And Kidogo smiled at PolePole. "But sometimes hurry hurry brings down breakfast." And PolePole grinned. "And sometimes slowly slowly finds a friend."